D1389364

For my son D.G.
and Ashby Willesley
Primary School
C.T.

For the children of
Bingham Kindergarten
S.G.

I Don't Want To!

Story by Sally Grindley
Pictures by Carol Thompson

Methuen Children's Books

When Mum came in and said
it was time to get up, James said,
"I don't want to,"
and hid himself under the sheets.

When Dad came up to help him
put on his brand new clothes,
James said, "I don't want to,"
and made himself all arms and legs.

When Mum gave him his egg and
said he must eat it before he went out,
James said, "I don't want to,"
and threw his soldiers on the floor.

When Dad put on his coat and
said it was time for them to go,
James said, "I don't want to."
But he had to.

"You'll enjoy it," said Dad.   "You'll have fun," said Mum.

"Won't," said James.

When they got into the car,
James said, "I want to go home."
When they drove up to the school,
James said, "I want to go home."

When they walked into the classroom,
James said, "I want to go home."
But he couldn't.
"Hello, James," said Miss Jones,
"come and sit with Jenny and Paul."
"I don't want to," said James.
"I want to go home."

"We're going to do some painting," said
Miss Jones. "Don't you want to join in?"
"No," said James, "I want to go home."

Miss Jones got out the paints and brushes.
The children put their aprons on.
    Miss Jones spread out a great big
frieze. The children started
to colour it in.

James sat still at his table and
tried very hard not to listen.
James sat still at his table and
tried very hard not to watch.
But he couldn't help thinking that
what they were doing looked fun.
He couldn't help wishing that
he was doing it too.

He couldn't help standing and
saying, "I want to do that."
Miss Jones was very pleased.

James joined in with the painting

and he joined in with the songs.

He joined in with the reading

and he joined in with the dance.

He joined in with the counting

and he joined in with the games.

When Mum came to collect him
and said it was time to go home,
James said, "I don't want to."
But he had to.

Then Miss Jones said,
"You can come back tomorrow."
The children said,
"Come back tomorrow."

And James wanted to.

First published in Great Britain in 1990
by Methuen Children's Books
a Division of The Octopus Publishing Group
Michelin House, 81 Fulham Road, London SW3 6RB
Text copyright © 1990 by Sally Grindley
Illustrations copyright © 1990 by Carol Thompson

Printed in Belgium
by Proost International Book Production

ISBN 0 416 13082 8